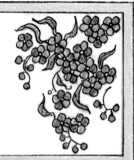

A WAS AN ANGLER

 ABC

DE FGH IJ

KL MNO PQ

RS TUV WX

 YZ

Janina Domanska

A WAS AN
ANGLER

GREENWILLOW BOOKS, NEW YORK

Watercolor paints, colored pencils, and a black pen were used for
the full-color art.   The text type is Veljovic Book.

Copyright © 1991 by Janina Domanska. All rights reserved. No part of this book
may be reproduced or utilized in any form or by any means, electronic or mechanical,
including photocopying, recording, or by any information storage and retrieval
system, without permission in writing from the Publisher, Greenwillow Books,
a division of William Morrow & Company, Inc., 105 Madison Avenue, New York, NY 10016.
Printed in Hong Kong by South China Printing Company (1988) Ltd.
First Edition   1 2 3 4 5 6 7 8 9 10

Library of Congress Cataloging-in-Publication Data

Domanska, Janina.
A was an angler / Janina Domanska.
p.   cm.
Summary: This nonsense rhyme, based on a
Mother Goose verse, introduces the letters from
A (Angler) to Z (Zebra).
ISBN 0-688-06990-8 (trade).
ISBN 0-688-06991-6 (lib. bdg.)
1. Nursery rhymes.   2. Alphabet rhymes.
3. Children's poetry.
[1. Nursery rhymes.   2. Alphabet.]
I. Title.   PZ8.3.D698Aaf   1991
398'.8—dc19   [e]   88-35589   CIP   AC

TO AVA, WITH LOVE

A was an angler,
Went out in a fog;
Who fish'd all the day,
And caught only a frog.

B was cook Betty,
A-baking a pie,
With ten or twelve apples
All piled up on high.

C was a custard
In a glass dish,
With as much cinnamon
As you could wish.

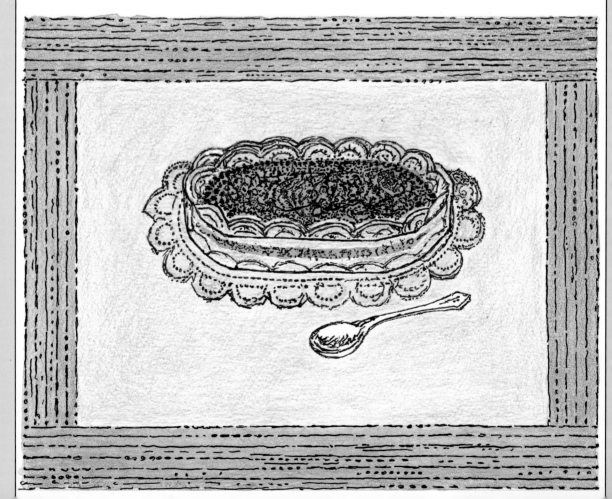

D

was fat Dick,
Who did nothing but eat;
He would leave book and play
For a nice bit of meat.

E was an egg,
In a basket with more,
Which Peggy will sell
For a shilling or more.

F was a fox,
So cunning and sly;
Who looks at the hen-roost—
I need not say why.

G was a greyhound,
As fleet as the wind;
In the race or the course,
Left all others behind.

H was a heron,
Who lived near a pond;
Of gobbling of fishes
He was wondrously fond.

I was the ice
On which Billy would skate;
So up went his heels,
And down went his pate.

J was Joe Jenkins,
Who played on the fiddle;
He began twenty times,
But left off in the middle.

K was a kitten,
who jumped at a cork,
And learned to eat mice
Without plate, knife, or fork.

L was a lark,
Who sings us a song,
And wakes us betimes
Lest we sleep too long.

M

was Miss Molly,
Who turned in her toes,
And hung down her head
Till her knees touched her nose.

N was a nosegay,
Sprinkled with dew,
Pulled in the morning
And presented to you.

O was an owl,
Who looked wondrously wise;
But he's watching a mouse
With his large round eyes.

P

was a parrot,
With feathers like gold,
Who talks just as much,
And knows more than he's told.

Q is the Queen,
Who governs the land,
And sits on a throne
Very lofty and grand.

R

is a raven
Perched on an oak,
Who with a gruff voice
Cries croak, croak, croak!

S was a stork
With a very long bill,
Who swallows down fishes
And frogs to his fill.

T is a trumpeter
Blowing his horn,
Who tells us the news
As we rise in the morn.

U is a unicorn,
Who, it is said,
Wears an ivory bodkin
On his forehead.

V

is a vulture,
Who eats a great deal,
Devouring a dog
Or a cat at a meal.

W
was a watchman,
Who guarded the street,
Lest robbers or thieves
The good people should meet.

X was King Xerxes,
Who, if you don't know,
Reigned over Persia
A great while ago.

Y

Y is the year
That is passing away,
And still growing shorter
Every day.

JANUARY
FEBRUARY
MARCH
APRIL
MAY
JUNE
JULY
AUGUST
SEPTEMBER
OCTOBER
NOVEMBER
DECEMBER

Z is a zebra,
Whom you've heard of before;
So here ends my rhyme
Till I find you some more.